Dear Parents and Educators,

Welcome to Penguin Young Readers! As parents and educators, you know that each child develops at his or her own pace—in terms of speech, critical thinking, and, of course, reading. Penguin Young Readers recognizes this fact. As a result, each Penguin Young Readers book is assigned a traditional easy-to-read level (1–4) as well as a Guided Reading Level (A–P). Both of these systems will help you choose the right book for your child. Please refer to the back of each book for specific leveling information. Penguin Young Readers features esteemed authors and illustrators, stories about favorite characters, fascinating nonfiction, and more!

A Is for Amber
Second Grade Rules, Amber Brown

LEVEL **3**

GUIDED READING LEVEL **K**

This book is perfect for a **Transitional Reader** who:
- can read multisyllable and compound words;
- can read words with prefixes and suffixes;
- is able to identify story elements (beginning, middle, end, plot, setting, characters, problem, solution); and
- can understand different points of view.

Here are some **activities** you can do during and after reading this book:
- Identify the problem in the story.
- Make Predictions: Will Amber win a Clean Desk Award?
- Toward the end of the story, Amber starts to dislike rules. The word *dislike* is made up of the prefix *dis-* and the root word *like*. On a separate sheet of paper, copy the chart below to list words you know that have prefixes.

Word	Prefix	Root Word
dislike	dis-	like

Remember, sharing the love of reading with a child is the best gift you can give!

—Bonnie Bader, EdM, and Katie Carella, EdM
    Penguin Young Readers program

*Penguin Young Readers are leveled by independent reviewers applying the standards developed by Irene Fountas and Gay Su Pinnell in *Matching Books to Readers: Using Leveled Books in Guided Reading*, Heinemann, 1999.

To Sheryl Hardin,
a valuable resource (and friend) for me
and a guiding light for her students. This
second-grade teacher rules!—PD

Penguin Young Readers
Published by the Penguin Group
Penguin Group (USA) Inc., 375 Hudson Street, New York, New York 10014, USA
Penguin Group (Canada), 90 Eglinton Avenue East, Suite 700, Toronto, Ontario M4P 2Y3, Canada
(a division of Pearson Penguin Canada Inc.)
Penguin Books Ltd., 80 Strand, London WC2R 0RL, England
Penguin Group Ireland, 25 St. Stephen's Green, Dublin 2, Ireland (
a division of Penguin Books Ltd.)
Penguin Group (Australia), 250 Camberwell Road, Camberwell, Victoria 3124, Australia
(a division of Pearson Australia Group Pty. Ltd.)
Penguin Books India Pvt. Ltd., 11 Community Centre, Panchsheel Park, New Delhi—110 017, India
Penguin Group (NZ), 67 Apollo Drive, Rosedale, Auckland 0632, New Zealand
(a division of Pearson New Zealand Ltd.)
Penguin Books (South Africa) (Pty.) Ltd., 24 Sturdee Avenue, Rosebank,
Johannesburg 2196, South Africa

Penguin Books Ltd., Registered Offices: 80 Strand, London WC2R 0RL, England

Text copyright © 2004 by Paula Danziger. Illustrations copyright © 2004 by Tony Ross. All rights
reserved. First published in 2004 by G. P. Putnam's Sons and in 2005 by Puffin Books, imprints of
Penguin Group (USA) Inc. Published in 2011 by Penguin Young Readers, an imprint of Penguin Group
(USA) Inc., 345 Hudson Street, New York, New York 10014. Manufactured in China.

The Library of Congress has cataloged the G. P. Putnam's Sons edition under
the following Control Number: 2003009340

ISBN 978-0-14-240421-8   10 9 8 7 6 5 4 3

PENGUIN YOUNG READERS

LEVEL 3
TRANSITIONAL READER

A IS FOR AMBER

Second Grade Rules, Amber Brown

by Paula Danziger
illustrated by Tony Ross

Penguin Young Readers
An Imprint of Penguin Group (USA) Inc.

It is a great second-grade day.

When I get to school,

Ms. Light beams at me.

She says that my math work

is getting better.

She helps me fix Bear Lee,

my backpack.

Bear Lee loves second grade.

So do I.

I am so happy.

Today is a great day.

My parents didn't yell
at each other this morning.
They've been doing that a lot lately, yelling.
It is my turn to read in the tree house.
I hope this is a great day forever.

"Bright Lights!"

Ms. Light claps her hands.

"Everyone, back to your desks."

I put a bookmark in the book

to remind me where I am.

Today is pocket day.

We count how many pockets

we each have.

I, Amber Brown, remembered.

And I am ready.

My blue overalls have seven pockets.

I show everyone my surprise.

I am wearing my red overalls

with six pockets under my blue ones.

That's thirteen pockets!

I am pocket queen.

I get to wear the crown all day.

"Second grade rules," I say,

sitting down next to

my best friend, Justin.

I think about that.

Second grade does rule.

It is the best.

And today, I am the queen.

Next is gym time.

Hannah Burton tries to trip me.

I win the race, anyway.

Our gym teacher, Ms. Van Winkle,

reminds Hannah about the rule

against tripping.

Next is snack time.

Ms. Light gives us snacks.

Yum.

I look around the room.

Ms. Light makes it look so magical.

Ms. Light does have some rules.

Always be respectful.

Be on time.

Do your own work.

Never say "I can't."

Always say "I'll try."

I, Amber Brown,

can deal with those rules.

I am not having any trouble

with second grade.

What can go wrong?

And then it happens.

It is terrible.

It is awful.

Ms. Light says,

"Class, I am adding a new rule today.

We have to keep our desks clean.

Some of you are getting out of control."

Ms. Light looks at me

when she says that.

I, Amber Brown,

am in trouble . . . big trouble.

I can't keep a neat desk.

I can't.

I know that I should say,

"I'll try," but I can't.

This rule is too hard for me.

Ms. Light says, "I just want you to know that the desk fairy will be coming to our room every once in a while.

She will leave treats and a Clean Desk Award—a shiny blue ribbon—on all the neat desks."

Tiffany Shroeder takes her thumb
out of her mouth.
She says, "I never heard of the
desk fairy."
Ms. Light acts shocked.
"You've never heard of the desk fairy?"
Tiffany shakes her head.
She puts her thumb back in her mouth.

"That's okay."

Ms. Light smiles.

"Her name is Deskarina.

She's a cousin of the tooth fairy."

Naomi Schwartz raises her hand.

"I have a cousin called Cindy," she says.

Everyone starts yelling out

the names of their cousins.

Ms. Light says,

"Listen to the story, class.

Deskarina's cousin, Dentalina,

already had the tooth fairy job.

Deskarina was jealous of Dentalina.

She heard about the desk fairy job.

She tried out for it . . . and she got

the job."

"Wow! I never knew the tooth fairy

had a name."

Naomi giggles.

"Everyone knows that," Hannah Burton says.

"But I would rather be a desk fairy and look in desks than be a tooth fairy and look in mouths . . . and touch other people's dirty teeth. That would be disgusting."

"My dad is a dentist," Fredrich says,

taking his finger out of his nose.

"It is good to touch other people's teeth."

I hope that Fredrich's father

is not a nose-picker like his son.

A nose-picking dentist . . . yuck.

Ms. Light says, "Use your imaginations
to write about and draw Deskarina."
I love doing this.
But a clean desk?
I don't know if I can do that.
I think about it—a Clean Desk Award.
I want one.
I write about Deskarina.
Then I draw her.
She is wearing a purple dress
and purple shoes.
She is wearing desk jewelry.
Her hair is pink, with glitter stars in it.
She's carrying a large backpack.
It's filled with treats and awards
for boys and girls with clean desks.

She also has notes in the backpack.

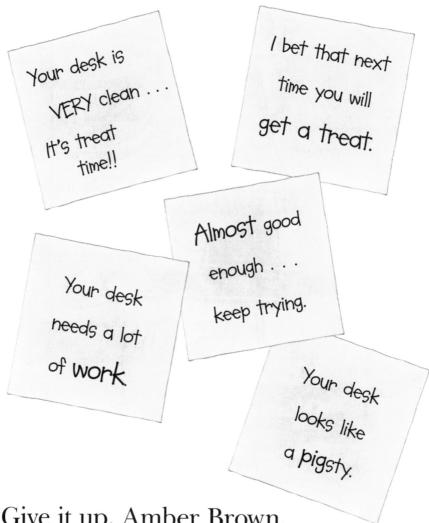

Your desk is VERY clean . . . It's treat time!!

I bet that next time you will get a treat.

Your desk needs a lot of work.

Almost good enough . . . keep trying.

Your desk looks like a pigsty.

Give it up, Amber Brown.

You will never get a treat.

Your desk should be named

a disaster zone.

I draw the Deskmobile.

Deskarina will drive it all over

the world, checking on desks.

It is much nicer than the tooth

fairy's vehicle, the Molar Express.

Lunch is next.

Justin and I share.

We dunk my potato chips

into his pudding.

I eat half of his peanut butter

and banana sandwich.

He eats half of my tuna fish sandwich.

He asks, "If a rooster lays an egg on a

slanted roof, will it roll to

the left or the right?"

I think about it.

I don't know.

Justin laughs and yells, "Neither.

Roosters don't lay eggs.

Chickens do."

Justin flaps his arms like a chicken
and makes chicken sounds.

Justin has decided that second grade
is the year of the chicken joke.

He is even thinking about
starting a chicken club.

It is time to go back to class.

I keep thinking about my desk.

How come some people have

no problem keeping their desks clean?

How come I can't?

I look in my desk.

It is filled with a lot of stuff.

I don't have time to clean it out.

Justin's mom is picking us up.

For the rest of the week,

I throw out one thing every day.

But, somehow, I put two more things in.

Deskarina does not come this week.

Next week, there is still no desk fairy.

I give up cleaning my desk.

If the fairy has trouble finding

our school, why should I bother?

And then it happens.

We all come into class.

There are ribbons and treats

on some desks.

Hannah Burton has them.

She acts so proud.

No one else in our group got any . . .

not Justin, not me, not Fredrich.

I look in my desk.

I see what Deskarina found . . .

five almost-empty potato chip

wrappers, a broken shoelace, seven

library books, a letter I was writing

to Aunt Pam, a crumpled page of

my book report, and six malted

milk balls covered with lint.

I guess Deskarina didn't think

my desk was clean enough.

I go home and tell my mom.

Mom tells me to practice

on my room.

She says it would be a treat . . .

for her . . . if we could find my

floor sometimes.

I should never have told Mom

about Deskarina.

I go to my room.

Cleaning is so boring.

I find my missing pink sock

with the silver glitter stars on it.

I thought that the washing

machine ate it.

I empty out a dresser drawer.

I pretend it is the inside of my desk.

Pencils here.

Pens there.

Extra scrunchies here.

Books there.

It seems easy.

I will do it at school.

I get to school.

Everyone is standing around

Bobby's desk.

He has brought his pet iguana,

Ike, to school.

I have to make a decision . . . meet

Ike or clean my desk.

I meet Ike.

Two days later, Deskarina visits again.

My desk is still messy.

This time Justin and Fredrich

and Hannah Burton get treats

from Deskarina.

I am so unhappy.

No ribbon for me.

Justin shares his treat with me.

But it is not the same as getting my own.

I, Amber Brown,

am beginning to dislike Deskarina.

Ms. Light says not to worry.

She sees improvement.

If I work a little harder,

she thinks Deskarina will see it, too.

I clean my desk during free time.

I put everything that I need in

my backpack.

For three days, I do not touch my desk.

I use my backpack.

Ms. Light says that I cannot do that.

I, Amber Brown,

am beginning to dislike rules.

But, I, Amber Brown,

really want a Clean Desk Award.

I can spell.

Why can't I keep my desk clean?

Even math is easier than keeping

my desk clean.

I keep trying.

Finally, I figure it out.

Instead of stuffing garbage in my desk,

I walk to the trash can.

It is boring to throw things out.

It is easier to just put them in my desk.

But I keep working at it.

Finally, my desk is clean.

Deskarina has not come back.

This time, I keep my desk clean.

It's amazing.

It is so much easier to find things.

Today, Justin and I are late.

My dad's car got a flat tire.

Class has already started.

We rush in.

People clap.

Even Ms. Light claps.

Tiffany points to my desk.

Deskarina was here last night.

She left me a treat . . .

and a ribbon.

I, Amber Brown,

have a Clean Desk Award!

I am so happy.

I wear my ribbon.

I share my treat with Justin.

He didn't get one this time.

Then I throw the used paper

in the trash can instead of in my desk.

Tonight I will put the ribbon
on my bulletin board in my room . . .
as soon as I find a place for it.